Geronimo Stilton
ENGLISH!

 **18 LET'S GO TO THE MOUNTAINS! 到山上去！**

U0061302

新雅文化事業有限公司
www.sunya.com.hk

Geronimo Stilton English
LET'S GO TO THE MOUNTAINS!　到山上去！

作　　者：Geronimo Stilton 謝利連摩·史提頓
譯　　者：申倩
責任編輯：王燕參
封面繪圖：Giuseppe Facciotto
插圖繪畫：Claudio Cernuschi, Andrea Denegri, Daria Cerchi
內文設計：Angela Ficarelli, Raffaella Picozzi
出　　版：新雅文化事業有限公司
　　　　　香港筲箕灣耀興道3號東匯廣場9樓
　　　　　營銷部電話：（852）2562 0161
　　　　　客戶服務部電話：（852）2976 6559
　　　　　傳真：（852）2597 4003
　　　　　網址：http://www.sunya.com.hk
　　　　　電郵：marketing@sunya.com.hk
發　　行：香港聯合書刊物流有限公司
　　　　　香港新界大埔汀麗路36號中華商務印刷大廈3字樓
　　　　　電話：（852）2150 2100　傳真：（852）2407 3062
　　　　　電郵：info@suplogistics.com.hk
印　　刷：C & C Offset Printing Co.,Ltd
　　　　　香港新界大埔汀麗路36號
版　　次：二〇一二年一月初版
　　　　　10 9 8 7 6 5 4 3 2 1

ISBN: 978-962-08-5494-1
© 2008 Edizioni Piemme S.p.A., Via Tiziano 32 - 20145 Milano - Italia
International Rights © 2007 Atlantyca S.p.A. - via Leopardi, 8, Milano - Italy
© 2012 for this Work in Traditional Chinese language, Sun Ya Publications (HK) Ltd.
9/F, Eastern Central Plaza, 3 Yiu Hing Rd, Shau Kei Wan, Hong Kong
Published and printed in Hong Kong

CONTENTS
目錄

BENJAMIN'S CLASSMATES
班哲文的老師和同學們

Maestra Topitilla
托比蒂拉・德・托比莉斯

Rarin
拉琳

Diego
迪哥

Rupa
露芭

Tui
杜爾

David
大衛

Sakura
櫻花

Mohamed
穆哈麥德

Tian Kai
田凱

Oliver
奧利佛

Milenko
米蘭哥

Trippo
特里普

Carmen
卡敏

Atina
阿提娜

Esmeralda
愛絲梅拉達

Pandora
潘朵拉

Takeshi
北野

Kuti
菊花

Benjamin
班哲文

Hsing
阿星

Laura
羅拉

Kiku
奇哥

Antonia
安東妮婭

Liza
麗莎

GERONIMO AND HIS FRIENDS
謝利連摩和他的家鼠朋友們

謝利連摩‧史提頓 Geronimo Stilton
一個古怪的傢伙，簡直可以說是一隻笨拙的文化鼠。他是
《鼠民公報》的總裁，正花盡心思改變報紙業的歷史。

菲‧史提頓 Tea Stilton
謝利連摩的妹妹，她是《鼠民公報》的特派記者，同
時也是一個運動愛好者。

班哲文‧史提頓 Benjamin Stilton
謝利連摩的小侄兒，常被叔叔稱作「我的
小乳酪」，是一隻感情豐富的小老鼠。

潘朵拉‧華之鼠 Pandora Woz
柏蒂‧活力鼠的姨甥女、班哲文最好的朋友，
是一隻活潑開朗的小老鼠。

柏蒂‧活力鼠 Patty Spring
美麗迷人的電視新聞工作者，致力於她熱愛的電視事業。

賴皮 Trappola
謝利連摩的表弟，非常喜歡食物，風趣幽默，是一隻饞
嘴、愛開玩笑的老鼠，善於將歡樂傳遞給每一隻鼠。

麗萍姑媽 Zia Lippa
謝利連摩的姑媽，對鼠十分友善，又和藹可親，只想將
最好的給身邊的鼠。

艾拿 Iena
謝利連摩的好朋友，充滿活力，熱愛各項運動，他希望
能把對運動的熱誠傳給謝利連摩。

史奎克‧愛管閒事鼠 Ficcanaso Squitt
謝利連摩的好朋友，是一個非常有頭腦的私家
偵探，總是穿着一件黃色的乾濕褸。

ON THE WAY   在路上

親愛的小朋友，你喜歡到山上去嗎？你喜歡樹林嗎？我兩樣都很喜歡呢！我愛樹林、清新的空氣、野生動物、漿果和藍莓……今天，我、柏蒂、班哲文和潘朵拉一起坐車到山上去，想知道我們在山上看見了什麼？快跟我們一起來吧！

What will we see?
我們會看見什麼？

跟我謝利連摩·史提頓一起學英文，就像玩遊戲一樣簡單好玩！

你可以一邊看着圖畫一邊讀。
以下有幾個標誌，你要特別留意：

🧀 當看到 💿 標誌時，你可以聽CD，一邊聽，一邊跟着朗讀，還可以跟着一起唱歌。

🧀 當看到 ⭐ 標誌時，你可以和朋友們一起玩遊戲，或者嘗試回答問題。題目很簡單，它們對鞏固你所學過的內容很有幫助。

🧀 當看到 ❗ 標誌時，你要注意看一下格子裏的生字，反覆唸幾遍，掌握發音。

最後，不要忘記完成小測驗和練習冊裏的問題！看看你有多聰明吧。

祝大家學得開開心心！

謝利連摩·史提頓

IN THE WOODS 在樹林裏

今天陽光燦爛，真是在林中散步的好日子。我們在樹林裏看見很多不同的動物和植物，班哲文和潘朵拉很想知道這些動植物的英文名稱，你也一起來學習吧！

woods

tree

path

glade

brushwood

What beautiful flowers! What are they called?

These are violets. Those are primroses!

violets

primroses

meadow

A PICNIC IN THE WOODS
在樹林裏野餐

我們在樹林裏找到了一片大草地,這裏真是野餐的好地方!我和柏蒂在草地上鋪好桌布後,班哲文和潘朵拉已急不及待幫忙拿出了所有食物。一起來看看我們帶了些什麼食物,並學習用英語說出這些食物的名稱吧!

water

bread   cheese

hamburger

pie

strawberries

juice

I like both raspberries and strawberries!

raspberries

berries

blueberries

blackberries

I prefer blueberries!

❗ both... and...
既……又……

I prefer...
我比較喜歡……

A SONG FOR YOU!

Track 1

Strawberries and Blueberries

Up in the mountains I'll go to the woods
to pick strawberries and blackberries.
I like raspberries and blueberries
and all kinds of berries,
I can't wait to eat them!
The berries are very good!
Very good!

FRIENDS OF THE WOODS
愛護樹林

我們一邊野餐，一邊欣賞風景。樹林真的很美麗，而且是一個豐富的寶藏，我們要好好愛護它。一起來看看我們在樹林裏要注意哪些事情吧！

Do not leave any rubbish in the woods.

Caution: do not light fires. A fire can destroy woods and kill animals.

Move quietly: animals get scared and hide when they hear a noise.

Respect the environment: do not pick flowers or mushrooms.

⭐ 試着用英語説出：「不要把垃圾留在樹林裏。」

答案：Do not leave any rubbish in the woods.

11

我們跟着導遊一邊參觀，一邊聽他介紹古時候的人們在城堡裏的生活是怎樣的……

A long time ago, in this castle…

used to 過去一向

The Lord of the castle and his Lady used to sit in this hall, next to the fireplace.

Banquets were held in the dancing hall.

The court jester used to tell funny stories to the Lord of the castle and his guests.

The musicians played while ladies and knights danced.

13

AT A HIGH ALTITUDE
從高處眺望

參觀完城堡後，我、柏蒂和孩子們決定去山頂看看。到了山頂，我們拿出望遠鏡向遠處望去，我以一千塊莫澤雷勒乳酪發誓，山頂四周的風景美麗極了！

mountains valley village pasture stream

dam artificial lake top / peak glacier pine

fir chalet cable cars

Look at that house at the bottom of the valley!

Look at the chalet on the top of that mountain!

❗ at the bottom of　在底部
on the top of　在頂部

The cable car takes us right to the peak, the highest point of the mountain.

★ 試着用英語説出以下詞彙：
村莊、冰川、纜車。

答案：village,
glacier, cable cars

MOUNTAIN ANIMALS
住在山裏的動物

我們乘坐纜車到另一座山去，在那裏我們看見了很多住在山裏的動物，班哲文和潘朵拉正仔細地聽着動物管理員的介紹，你也一起來學習吧！

bear
marmot
eagle
antelope
blackbird
deer
crow
viper
weasel

Bears are carnivores.

Marmots are rodents.

Eagles have broad wings and strong claws.

Antelopes are very agile and jump from one rock to another.

wings　翅膀
claws　爪子

HIKING 遠足

每年夏季，山上的風景都特別怡人，最適合去遠足了。遠足需要很多裝備，一起來學習怎樣用英語說出這些物品的名稱吧！

trousers

shirt

climbing boots

fleece sweater

hat

waterproof jacket

anorak

rucksack

tent

sleeping bag

⭐ 去遠足時，應該帶些什麼食物？試着用英語説説看。

17

SKIING 滑雪

每年冬季，山上都會變成一片雪白，成為滑雪愛好者的好去處。看，班哲文已急不及待穿上滑雪屐去滑雪了。滑雪也需要很多裝備，一起來學習怎樣用英語說出這些物品的名稱吧！

snowsuit

sweatshirt

quilted jacket

poles

skis

boots

snow boots

sledge / sleigh

bobsled

snowboard

ski goggles

gloves

We'll go on the sledge...

... and on the bobsled!

I'll have skiing lessons.

I'll take the cable car and go on top!

I'm very happy to have come on this trip!

Wait Uncle G, I'll take a picture of you!

I Love Going to the Mountains

I love the winter, when the snow falls
I'll go skiing, I'll take the ropeway
I'll take the cable car or the ski-lift
up to the top of the mountains.
I love going to the mountains
I like the snow, I like skiing.
It's beautiful in the mountains
when the sun is shining.
I take my sweater and my sunglasses with me
I'll also take my camera to take pictures with
I'll take something to eat, too
and when I'm hungry I'll go to eat in the chalet.
I love going to the mountains
I like the snow, I like skiing.
It's beautiful in the mountains
when the sun is shining.

〈刻在石牆上的畫〉

謝利連摩接到一個神秘電話，告訴他在離妙鼠城不遠的一個山洞裏找到了一幅刻在石牆上的畫。

謝利連摩：他們在電話裏說那些畫就在這個山洞裏。

柏蒂：謝利連摩，如果這是真的，那將會是世紀獨家新聞。

班哲文：謝利連摩叔叔，我實在太興奮了！

謝利連摩：哦，它們真的在這裏！

柏蒂：這個發現將會改寫妙鼠城的整個歷史。

班哲文：根據這些古老的壁畫，妙鼠城以前住滿了長毛象。

潘朵拉：看，最後一隻還穿了裙子呢！

班哲文：來吧。我們快點去報道這則獨家新聞吧！

柏蒂：等一等，班哲文，可能……

謝利連摩：啊，小孩子總是這麼性急。

第二天……

記者：我可以跟你做個訪問嗎？

〔一把聲音說〕真是一則偉大的報道！

〔一把聲音說〕這個發現其實是一個騙局！！！

柏蒂：什麼？

謝利連摩和柏蒂：莎莉·尖刻鼠！

莎莉：各位先生女士，這位是卡文娜·淘古鼠教授，是妙鼠城大自然故事博物館的館長。教授，請你告訴他們……

卡文娜：我的朋友謝利連摩，很對不起，但那些畫……

卡文娜：……是假的！

莎莉：假的！這則獨家新聞只是一個謊言。

I called this conference to apologise and explain what happened.

兩個小時後，在《鼠民公報》大樓的會議室裏……
謝利連摩：我召開這個會議的目的是想跟大家道歉和解釋一下整件事。

We were wrong. We thought those graffiti were authentic.

謝利連摩：我們弄錯了，我們以為那些畫是真實的！

I would like to congratulate Sally Rasmaussen.

謝利連摩：但我要恭喜莎莉·尖刻鼠。

One of the mammoths was wearing a skirt...

謝利連摩：其中一隻長毛象穿了裙子……

... made from the material missing from this jacket!

She is the author of those phoney graffiti!

You got me, Stilton!

Hooray for Geronimo Stilton!

The End

謝利連摩：而那裙子正好與莎莉這件外套上缺少的部分一樣。她就是繪畫這些畫的作者。
莎莉：竟然被你抓到我的破綻，史提頓！
記者：為謝利連摩歡呼！

TEST 小測驗

⭐ 1. 用英語說出下面的動物名稱。

 (a)
 (b)
 (c)
 (d)

狼　　　　　　鼴鼠　　　　　　鹿　　　　　　臭鼬鼠

⭐ 2. 用英語說出下面的句子。

(a) 我既喜歡藍莓又喜歡士多啤梨。
I love both ... and ... .

(b) 我比較喜歡黑莓。
I prefer ... .

⭐ 3. 用英語說出下面的標語。

(a) 不要留下垃圾！Do not ... ... !
(b) 不要生火！ Do not ... ... !
(c) 不要摘花！Do not ... ... !

⭐ 4. 用英語說出下面的詞彙。

 (a)
 (b)
 (c)
 (d)

山　　　　　　山谷　　　　　　溪流　　　　　　村莊

⭐ 5. 用英語說出下面的句子。

(a) 羚羊非常敏捷。
... are very ... .

(b) 鷹有寬闊的翅膀。
... have broad ... .

24

DICTIONARY 詞典

（英、粵、普發聲）

A

agile　敏捷

altitude　高處

animals　動物

anorak　禦寒外套

antelope　羚羊

artificial lake　人工湖

B

banquets　宴會

bear　熊

berries　莓果

blackberries　黑莓

blackbird　畫眉

blueberries　藍莓

boar　公豬

bobsled　大雪橇

boots　靴子

bread　麵包

brushwood　草叢

butterfly　蝴蝶

C

cable cars　纜車

carnivores　肉食動物

castle　城堡

caution　小心

cave　山洞

chalet　瑞士的農舍

cheese　乳酪

claws　爪子

climbing boots　爬山鞋

conference　會議

crow　烏鴉

D

dam　水壩

dancing hall　跳舞廳

dangerous 危險

deer 鹿

destroy 破壞

dormouse 睡鼠

drawbridge 吊橋

E

eagle 鷹

environment 環境

F

fawn 小鹿

fir 杉樹

fireplace 壁爐

fleece sweater 抓毛衞衣

fox 狐狸

G

get scared 使害怕

glacier 冰川

glade 林間空地

gloves 手套

H

hamburger 漢堡包

hare 野兔

hat 帽子

hedgehog 刺蝟

hiking 遠足

history 歷史

I

interview 訪問

J

juice 果汁

K

kill 殺死

knights 武士

M

marmot 土撥鼠

meadow 草地

moat 護城河

mole　鼴鼠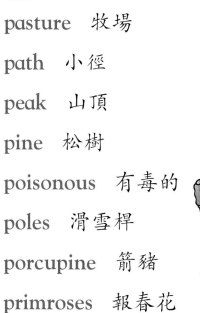

mountains　山

mushrooms　蘑菇

O

owl　貓頭鷹

P

pasture　牧場

path　小徑

peak　山頂

pine　松樹

poisonous　有毒的

poles　滑雪桿

porcupine　箭豬

primroses　報春花

Q

quilted jacket　棉襖

R

raspberries　木莓

rucksack　背包

S

safe　安全

shirt　恤衫（普：襯衫）

ski goggles　滑雪護目鏡

skiing　滑雪

skirt　裙子

skis　滑雪屐

skunk　臭鼬鼠

sledge　雪橇

sleeping bag　睡袋

sleigh　雪橇

snow boots　雪靴

snowboard　滑雪板

snowsuit　雪衣

squirrel　松鼠

strawberries　士多啤梨

　（普：草莓）

stream　溪流

sweatshirt　長袖運動衫

T

tent 帳篷

ticket office 售票處

tower 塔樓

tree 樹

trick 騙局

trousers 長褲

wolf 狼

woodpecker 啄木鳥

woods 樹林

V

valley 山谷

village 村莊

violets 紫羅蘭

viper 毒蛇

W

walls 城牆

water 水

waterproof jacket
　防水外套

weasel 黃鼠狼

wings 翅膀

看在一千塊莫澤雷勒乳酪的份上，你學得開心嗎？很開心，對不對？好極了！跟你一起跳舞唱歌我也很開心！我等着你下次繼續跟班哲文和潘朵拉一起玩一起學英語呀。現在要說再見了，當然是用英語說啦！

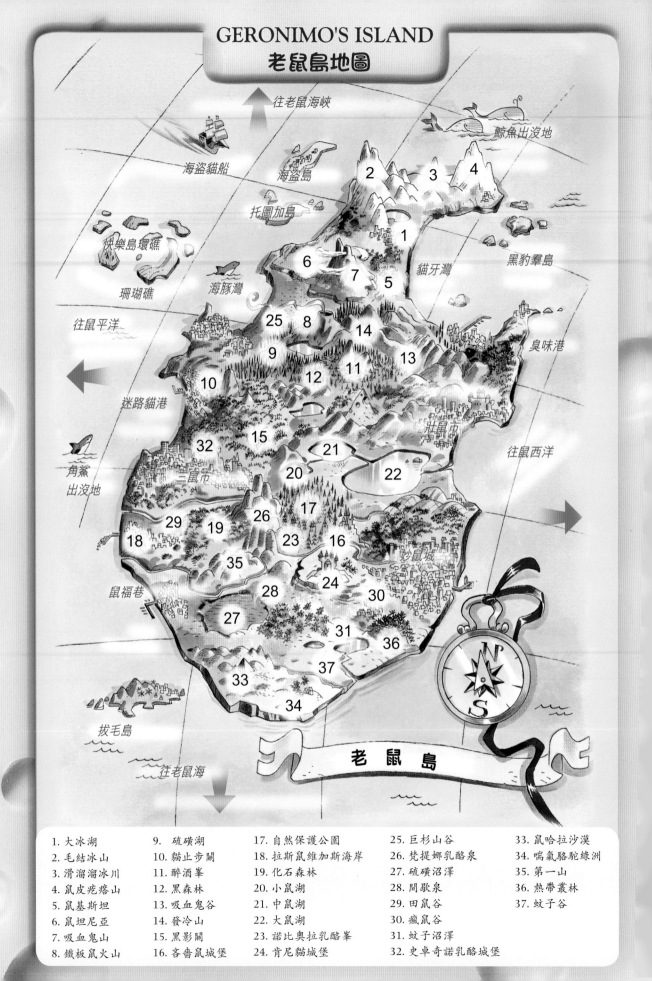

GERONIMO'S ISLAND
老鼠島地圖

往老鼠海峽

鯨魚出沒地

海盜貓船

海盜島

托圖加島

快樂島環礁

珊瑚礁

海豚灣

往鼠平洋

黑豹羣島

貓牙灣

臭味港

往鼠西洋

迷路貓港

角鯊
出沒地

壯鼠市

三鼠市

妙鼠城

鼠福巷

拔毛島

往老鼠海

老鼠島

1. 大冰湖	9. 硫磺湖	17. 自然保護公園	25. 巨杉山谷	33. 鼠哈拉沙漠
2. 毛結冰山	10. 貓止步關	18. 拉斯鼠維加斯海岸	26. 梵提娜乳酪泉	34. 喘氣駱駝綠洲
3. 滑溜溜冰川	11. 醉酒峯	19. 化石森林	27. 硫磺沼澤	35. 第一山
4. 鼠皮疙瘩山	12. 黑森林	20. 小鼠湖	28. 間歇泉	36. 熱帶叢林
5. 鼠基斯坦	13. 吸血鬼谷	21. 中鼠湖	29. 田鼠谷	37. 蚊子谷
6. 鼠坦尼亞	14. 發冷山	22. 大鼠湖	30. 瘋鼠谷	
7. 吸血鬼山	15. 黑影關	23. 諾比奧拉乳酪峯	31. 蚊子沼澤	
8. 鐵板鼠火山	16. 客嗇鼠城堡	24. 肯尼貓城堡	32. 史卓奇諾乳酪城堡	

Geronimo Stilton

EXERCISE BOOK
練習冊

想知道自己對 LET'S GO TO THE MOUNTAINS! 掌握了多少，
趕快打開後面的練習完成它吧！

ENGLISH!

18 LET'S GO TO THE MOUNTAINS! 到山上去！

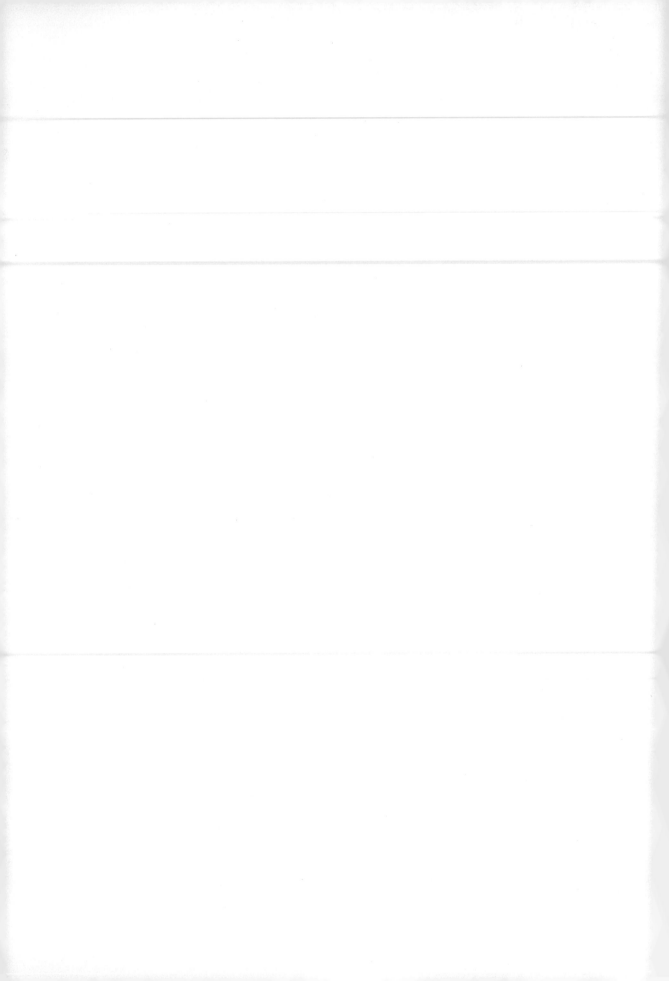

ON THE WAY　在路上

⭐ 謝利連摩、柏蒂、班哲文和潘朵拉準備去哪裏？看看他們的對話，然後選出適當的詞彙填在橫線上，你就會知道了。

> will　　　　see　　　　going　　　　walk

2. What _____ we see, Uncle G?

1. We are _____ to the mountains! Wonderful!

3. We'll _____ the Toma Mountains, woods, animals.

4. And we'll _____ up to the peak!

IN THE WOODS 在樹林裏

⭐ 樹林裏住着很多動物，你知道牠們的英文名稱嗎？根據提示，在橫線上寫出各種動物的名稱。

提示：mole   deer   skunk
        dormouse   wolf   porcupine

1.

_____

2.

_____

3.

_____

4.

_____

5.

_____

6.

_____

A PICNIC IN THE WOODS
在樹林裏野餐

★ 你還記得謝利連摩他們帶了些什麼食物去野餐嗎？在橫線上寫出缺少的英文字母，然後給圖畫填上適當的顏色吧。

1. h__mb__rger

2. w__t__r

3. ch__es__

4. p__ __

5. br__ __d

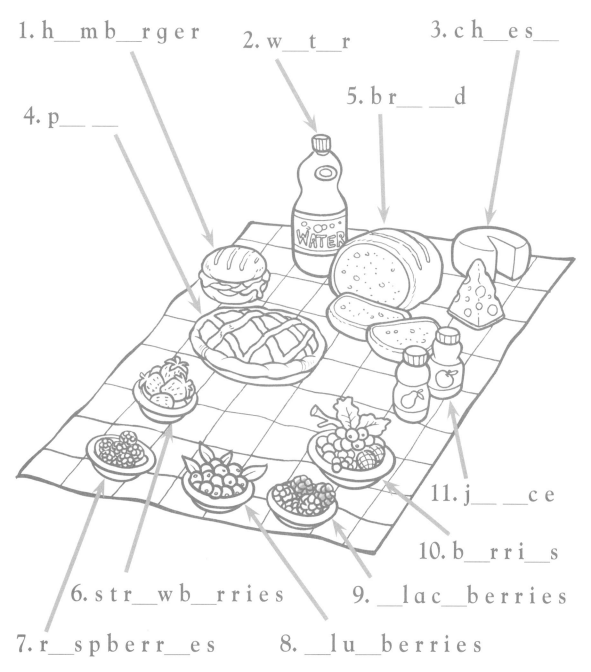

11. j__ __ce

10. b__rri__s

6. str__wb__rries

9. __lac__berries

7. r__spberr__es

8. __lu__berries

FRIENDS OF THE WOODS
愛護樹林

⭐ 我們應該怎樣愛護樹林呢？根據提示，選出正確的詞彙填在橫線上，完成句子。

提示：woods   rubbish   animals   noise
Respect   fires   mushrooms

1. Do not leave any _____
   in the woods!

2. Caution: do not light _____ .
A fire can destroy _____ and kill _____ .

3. Move quietly: animals get scared and hide
   when they hear a _____ .

4. _____ the environment:
   do not pick flowers or _____ .

4

A VISIT TO THE CASTLE
參觀城堡

⭐ 看看下面的圖畫，根據提示，在橫線上寫出城堡的各個部分。

提示： drawbridge
tower   merlons
moat   walls

1. _____

2. _____

3. _____

4. _____

5. _____

A LONG TIME AGO, IN THE CASTLE...
很久以前，在城堡裏……

⭐ 你知道古時候的人們在城堡裏的生活是怎樣的嗎？根據圖畫，選出正確的詞彙填在橫線上，完成句子。

played	danced	sit	tell

1. The Lord of the castle and his Lady used to _____ in this hall.

2. The court jester used to _____ funny stories to the Lord of the castle and his guests.

3. The musicians _____ while ladies and knights _____ .

MOUNTAIN ANIMALS
住在山裏的動物

★ 山裏住着很多動物，你知道牠們的英文名稱嗎？根據提示，在橫線上寫出各種動物的名稱。

提示：crow   marmot   eagle   weasel
       deer   bear   viper

1. _____

2. _____

3. _____

4. _____

5. _____

6. _____

7. _____

ANSWERS 答案

TEST 小測驗

1. (a) wolf   (b) mole   (c) deer   (d) skunk
2. (a) I love both <u>blueberries</u> and <u>strawberries</u>.   (b) I prefer <u>blackberries</u>.
3. (a) Do not <u>leave any rubbish</u>!   (b) Do not <u>light fires</u>!   (c) Do not <u>pick flowers</u>!
4. (a) mountains   (b) valley   (c) stream   (d) village
5. (a) <u>Antelopes</u> are very <u>agile</u>.   (b) <u>Eagles</u> have broad <u>wings</u>.

EXERCISE BOOK 練習冊

P.1

1. going   2. will   3. see   4. walk

P.2

1. wolf   2. deer   3. porcupine   4. mole   5. dormouse   6. skunk

P.3

1. h<u>a</u>mb<u>u</u>rger   2. w<u>a</u>t<u>e</u>r   3. ch<u>ee</u>s<u>e</u>   4. p<u>ie</u>   5. br<u>ea</u>d
6. str<u>a</u>wb<u>e</u>rries   7. r<u>a</u>spb<u>e</u>rr<u>ie</u>s   8. <u>b</u>l<u>ue</u>berries   9. <u>b</u>l<u>a</u>c<u>k</u>berries
10. b<u>e</u>rr<u>ie</u>s   11. j<u>ui</u>ce

P.4

1. rubbish   2. fires, woods, animals   3. noise   4. Respect, mushrooms

P.5

1. tower   2. merlons   3. drawbridge   4. walls   5. moat

P.6

1. sit   2. tell   3. played, danced

P.7

1. bear   2. eagle   3. marmot   4. deer
5. crow   6. viper   7. weasel